Diary of the Knuckle Head Street Child

Quinche Tucker

Diary of the Knuckle Head Street Child

Olympia Publishers
London

www.olympiapublishers.com
OLYMPIA PAPERBACK EDITION

Copyright © Quinche Tucker 2024

The right of Quinche Tucker to be identified as author of
this work has been asserted in accordance with sections 77 and 78 of
the Copyright, Designs and Patents Act 1988.

All Rights Reserved

No reproduction, copy or transmission of this publication
may be made without written permission.
No paragraph of this publication may be reproduced,
copied or transmitted save with the written permission of the publisher,
or in accordance with the provisions
of the Copyright Act 1956 (as amended).

Any person who commits any unauthorized act in relation to
this publication may be liable to criminal
prosecution and civil claims for damage.

A CIP catalogue record for this title is
available from the British Library.

ISBN: 978-1-80439-432-8

This is a work of fiction.
Names, characters, places and incidents originate from the writer's
imagination. Any resemblance to actual persons, living or dead, is
purely coincidental.

First Published in 2024

Olympia Publishers
Tallis House
2 Tallis Street
London
EC4Y 0AB

Printed in Great Britain

Dedication

I dedicate this book to my loving Mother who stands like a soldier, Janice Marie Laster.

Acknowledgements

Thank you, Datroon Tyrun Hammond, Zavere Morshawn Smith, Byntlee Chenelle Bell my brothers Lee Beasley and Quinn Tucker.

"Time shares the same experience of change just as the moment, may your mind be in hot pursuit."

Knuckle Head Street Child

I'm seventeen now; I guess too much for mama. She says, I talk back too much. She says, I'm just like my daddy, she says, what you gone do boy, holding ya nuts too heavy round here, without paying a bill. I say, all right... I'm gone. Head down stepping out, slammed the door, Fuck it, I'm out here.

My days have been spent wondering and sneaking around. My wonders of why people keep running around saying life's a Blessing, I don't know... I mean let me see... smiling, my mom and little sister Blessings (punching the wall), why the Fuck she says I had to leave! Closing my eyes, if life is such a Blessing and death so tragic, then why is it that I'm now looking for a blessed death living my tragic life.

My mind is racing today, trying hard not to catch no case, just for food, man people don't realize most drug dealers don't start off for the glam, shit we be hungry, shoes ain't right, shower needed, basic needs wrapped around Broke Dreams and constant bullshit. I'm tryna figure out how to keep Dreams alive. I'm Broke and Broken, who can help me, without shaming me.

I keep my diary with me, so I make sure my inside feelings are never exposed to the world. I mean they exposed through the raft I bring to these streets. Three months in the game, money still in short comings ten-dollar bags of green ain't shit, but my come up is real. I tell my Big Homie when he kicks down his lyrics, that he can spit about flushing twenties down the toilet and that's cool cause that's where he at in life, but me shit I'll whoop some ass over a twenty... different levels in life. He laughs calling me desperate, maybe I am. Desperate for what, this money, let me check, nah not that, my heart, yelp that's the match Dam! Mama, Mama, Mom.

I'm feeling good almost eighteen and no record... who that knocking on the door... hold on I'll be right back, let me hide my shit under my nut sack, these suckas ain't gone get me...

Two weeks in Juvenile Detention for unlawful delivery. Just now being able to get back to you, guards bout threw you away, but you were saved, did I say saved, I meant safe. I can take care of me but you, can't deal without me, I watched you shake with fear when we departed. Shaking like a little boy wanting a hug from mama, hold me mama, where you at, you still mad. I'm trying when I say my brain defines it as hustling... that's trying right... Am I trying or not?

Happy thanks giving! my homeboy yells, tapping me on the shoulder. I wake get dressed, and head to my grandmama house, my sister was there and my mom. I made eye contact with my mom, but she quickly moved her eyes combined with shaking her head. Why she acts like that? I don't know, I don't get it. Parents kill me with this, get ya shit together attitude toward their kids. I have been in the world for eighteen years take eight away and wasn't long ago. I was just a ten-year-old child. Parents don't have it all together and they be forty and up.

I know this because they are always asking, what you gone do, instead of knowing how to help you Strengthen the Good that you are already showing. Remind me of the Good that I have done, show me, and Help me Hold on to that so I can Grow and be Strong.

Tell me mama, what did you Love about me, I need to hold on to that Goodness, put that in your mouth, nourish me. Mom! What is it? Rock me, rock me, just for a little bit...

My heart skipped a beat when I saw the girl of my life, she was sitting right outside the corner store. I couldn't believe that she was staring at me. I smiled a quick smile, she was cute. I walked quickly. I was thinking, as I was looking at my jeans, dam I'm happy she didn't recognize the stains I wore on my jeans. Loyalty runs deep for me, I wonder can she see my Worth through my Smile, or will her decision be determined off my Gear? She gone keep stepping? I got that number! I was happy when she took mine. Her worth I cannot measure right now, but opportunity is well defined.

Long night phone calls, laughing as she tells me about her future. "What about you?" She asks. I laugh and I reply "chillin'." The safest reply to have when you fear not having anything to say good enough to stamp her heart. Questioning what I want in life would be a repetitive part of our conversation except now after amazing sex. I'm wondering if this was her first assignment, measuring my worthiness through my stroke action.

Hold up Little Dude, what you mean you short on my money, shit ain't adding up, you told me you would have that extra fifty bucks. I need that for a place to stay tonight.

Fuck! I ain't no bitch, so you not gone see me write no bunch of "I can't see the way out," type bullshit, cause that's a waste of time. I snatched the last three $10 bags of trees from bruh, dam dude dang. I don't know what the hell I'm posed to do now, you out here playing... remember... you got a place to stay.

I walked into a place familiar to what I have been missing, only to be greeted by sadness. His mom welcomes me, giving me a place to lay my head and I am thankful for that. I know longer stay there. I am Temporary, Am I Temporary? The love people have for me... Temporary.

My arms are tired as I drag the wheels to my suitcase down the road. The sun has my armpits talking to me as the smell enters the bus, heads turn, noses frown up. I ain't tripping, these same looks appear on the face of the world. Ghetto Bastard. I scramble through my pocket to assure the three $10.00 bags are still there. I step out the bus.

I am content to see my girlfriend standing there, she accepts me, she loves me, she's not mine. I reached out to her, she leaned into the arms of the man that can provide. Grabbing the railing of the bus as she steps in, I step out. I turn back to look one last time, hoping she might change her mind. The word Hope has left me disappointed too many times. I've exchanged the word Hope for the word Dope, and this begins my journey into what would become the next part of my life.

The food from the Soup Kitchen matches the sour smell of the clothes on my back. I dig in my pocket to light and inhale the last few drags of my cigarette, leaned up against the convenient store. The heat of the sun on my face was interrupted by a shadow of darkness. I quickly look up; the man stands looking at me. The man says, "You Good," I reply shrugging my shoulders, "I guess." I can help you bruh, come fuck with me, down on Luther and fifteenth. The man reaches out, I'm Big T, "here go twenty dollars," get you something to eat.

I spend a lot of time getting to know Big T, always full of jokes, keeps me laughing. He whispered the importance of staying clean, only into my ears. He never allows any of his friends to tease me, my life has changed since I met Big T, he is truly a friend.

Many of my days are spent perfecting the craft of cutting, packaging with a combination of dodging one time (police) for the ones that don't know. Pleased with the come up, I started looking drippy on the outside but still sad on the inside. Mama… Mama… Mama can you hear me.

The smell of pussy fills the air as (ass) strippers danced around the hotel room, where Big T, Little Marshall and I stood in the amazement! Big T and I are used to strippers and what they bring, but Little Marshall wants the instant gratification, so we entrusted him with the name Headhunter. In the blink of an eye, he was out the room getting head in somebody's vehicle. I say somebody cause the nearest smoker that has a car, he has the product, and the trade occurs. Marshall's game would lead him into a world of baby mamas, drug addiction and a few years in… hold up. I'll be right back. Okay I'm back motherfuckas was knocking on my motel door, wasn't nobody, wrong door.

Back to Marshall, my boy gone, he locked up I write him when I can. I know he must be lonely, I wish he had a close friend, like I have in you. I don't have to worry, you won't leave me or change your tone toward me, a place that will shelter me from this mean world, something that does not have the power to leave me, leave you, leave us.

Jazmin's lips are amazing. I stare at them as she talks to me about life, I really like my new girlfriend. I spend time looking for a place to call ours, as I spend most nights climbing in and out of her bedroom window. Caressing her body on the bed, while sleeping underneath it.

I hear the creeks on her wood floor, as her father comes near. She grown, but her stubborn ways have trapped her in a home, where privilege stands to protect her from the ugly scars of unfortunates.

I laugh as she rushes to put perfume in the air, so her love for sex isn't revealed to the honorable up bringing her father has worked so hard to shelter his families title around. She looks under the bed, "Coast Clear" she says. I grab my shoes and pants and flee the scene. The scene of what the accident she is pregnant.

Jazmin pushes my baby in the world today. I close my eyes to picture the lonely girl she must have been and currently may be, not knowing where the man had gone that planted a seed in the womb, left to grow, as if to be unworthy of the creator.

I sat outside the hospital writing, the only true place of my acceptance. The smell of my sour clothes and tainted look distracts and disturbs my motivation to walk through the sliding doors of the hospital.

I scramble to my phone as it rings, my grandmother is calling me, "Boy, that girl dun had that baby, betta get up there!" Walking through the doors and peeking in the room, the anticipation of rejection, surprising enough did not push me out the way. Her beautiful strong dark brown hand welcomes me, and the little tender hands that we created reached out from under those blankets to say, come here daddy you are loved.

My head begins to spin not knowing what to do or how to react, I have nothing to give her, I am drained of hope, I am empty handed reaching for the remote as I sit in the hospital room. I can't stand it much longer, as I kiss her soft skin and walk out the room. I have a child that will start off not knowing who I am, but I can't allow her to remain a child with no father, not another Bastard Child, yes me not her, not we, not again.

Big T and Little Marshall, kick in the celebration to my big eighteen. I don't know why Big T seem so consistent in raining down on every female that comes to the party. Comments like, she ain't shit, she worth a lil bit of nothing, as he takes a second look at Big Booty Rita and says "She sho at shit." I guess the accident has left him with a hardened heart toward what he already knows doesn't bring attraction to the eye.

Little Marshall, tipsy from the Hennessey replaces the empty space of sadness that hides within me and provides comfort that confronts the heart of Big T, as he yells out "My boy legs may not work, but his dick still do!" Me and Big T bust out laughing this dude is stupid, Marshall continues, "Come on girl get on my boy!" Tina runs through the crowd, giving Big T a lap dance, that even captures my attention. I enjoyed all the laughter that filled the room this evening.

The sun kissed my brown skin as if to send a message of wanted intimacy. I held my head back closed my eyes to give reassurance that it would happen. The sun kiss made me remember that today is my mother's birthday. I sprang up interrupting my intimate moment and scrolled through my phone to find her number. The mighty thump in my chest gave a mighty push toward each ring that preceded the possibility of my mother answering the phone. She answered the phone and the quietness that shares our voices continues to reign over the relationship we have.

Mom and I laugh as she describes her attempts to still kick down the Funky Chicken dance. My heart was so anxiously trying to convince my mouth to open and ask her if she still loves me, ever wondered how I was doing, or even checked the funeral portion of the local newspaper to see if she may had missed out on my funeral. The thought was quickly interrupted when my sister snatched the phone and asked to see me, I agreed to meet her, she handed the phone back to my mom. Hey, Mama... do you ever... Nah never mind.

I left the park feeling happy that I got to sit and talk to my sister, it was great listening and watching her express how she won her softball game. The cheering in her voice, as she demonstrated how she ran up and grabbed that "hot" ball, releasing it like the pistol of a ghetto child, as she got the last out, winning the game! I wanted to go, I will go, I won't embarrass you with the smell that comes from my clothes... I wanna know... well I wish I...

I was in the middle of grabbing the last breakfast plate they had available at the Soup Kitchen this morning, when a hand grabbed mine, a familiar touch of distance. I looked up to see, who I call, "the man that fell victim to the raft in my heart...my father. There he stood six ft. five black as the hearts of past presidents. He extended an invitation for me to come and stay with him. Days and nights would fall as I slept on his couch, appreciating a place to stay. I exchanged the sewer rats for cock roaches, I didn't complain.

The swaying of her hips as she walked back and forth to the kitchen was only of temporary arousal, for she was my father's girlfriend and off limits. Eye connection and lingering nights of conversation along with my father dedication to gin, created the perfect sin. The creation presented opened access for his responsibility to be placed on me, the declaration was made, evidenced by her legs crossing over my lap.

A light tap on my shoulder early one morning came from my father, looking at me with his bold eyes, that seem to demand my attention, like the Buffalo Soldiers when the U.S. tried to wrap up their importance to exist. The dark makeup that stained my white shirt along with my underwear lying naked and alone on the floor, motioned my father to speak, a man of little words. He spoke "It's time to go, this house ain't big enough for the both of us," already packing my bags, its two a.m.

Saturday morning wind always seems to prove its power and dominance over any other time of day. The weeds are giving my ankles a spanking on this morning as Big T walks me across the grassy fields to fish for the first time. Here, dude dang, as Big T showed me how to hook the worm. I smacked my lips a few times and rolled my eyes, shit seemed a bit boring for a minute. I begin to slowly witness the trees waving and the running river, so blessed with the presence of the sun. The lake has taking my breath and cradled my soul.

I never said anything to him, but I recognized the side

smile he gave, watching the excitement I experienced when catching my first fish! I have been introduced to a Peace I have never found, Mothers' Nature.

Little Marshall threw a pillow at my dome, that woke me up. "Man, ya phone been ringing nonstop, messing with my beauty sleep." Jazmin was calling to talk to me about how fast the baby was growing, and the clothes she once could wear, she has now outgrown. A loud piercing rings in my ear with such force I just hang up! Not this shit, I can't let this shit happen, she needs me, I want her to always need me, my daughter.

Sitting here at the lake that has secretly captured my love, keeps the darkness from taken me captive, into a mindset where I just don't give a fuck. I sit and find myself gazing at the water, as my stomach begs for my attention, anxiously waiting for the doors to open at the Soup Kitchen. I recognize that I am sharing the lake with a man and what appears to be his son. He has caught me in the middle of observing his interaction with this child. I don't want him to think I'm in his business. I look up to notice the boy using a stepping stick to lead the way, and every other step he appeared to take a deep breath looking toward the sky. I wonder is he inhaling the same peace that still lingers in my lungs the moment I stepped foot on this land. A voiced called out, "Hey come here," I'm not going to reply because I don't think the voice is for me, again the voice called out "Hey come here." I realize that he is talking to me, I wonder what he wants, I'll be back... hold on.

I know I kept you waiting longing then you expected in the hot sun, my fault. I must share with you, in this moment I can't leave from this lake without filling you in on this moment, it wouldn't be fair to you, recognizing the tears that flow down my face. I think I have just walked in the same space as Freedom, not yet enough confidence to have a seat.

The making of the moment was created from the second he looked at me. I never got to ask his name which stands for little importance compared to the gift he delivered. My voice which usually drives conversations, for some reason stood at attention, in strict silence this morning.

The fisherman's request for me to unhook the snag in the fishing line that stood between a rock and a tree branch was very confusing. I could see that he had a boy with him, that looked about twelve years of age, and wondered why he couldn't do it.

The fisherman sparked his conversation around the love he has for bringing his son to a place of peace. In further observation of the boy, I recognized a gloss that blanketed his eyes and once again encountered the walking stick, the combination of the two gave clarity to his blindness. The boy turned his head after hearing his father's voice and struggled to grab the walking stick that eventually assisted him in standing to his feet. The name is Sam, he expressed as he pierced the worm through his hook, my son was born blind and death, so it's takes him a little longer to catch on to things.

His mother looked at him and decided if God was going to send her a child in these conditions, that she was not going to wait until it was her natural time to go be with the Lord to ask him why. She left one night, came back and I found her dead with a needle in her arm. Look, I gotta go right now, I'll be back tomorrow.

Diary, you have sheltered and now taking the place of my past tears, pain and hurt. These tears I shed as I speak, have been freed from the bondage of you. My eyes have reclaimed my tears, for the first time. I am having an intimate experience with True Trust.

Sam and I are building trust that gives my new tears permission to fall from my eyes and not have to fear the quick swipe of my hand. My tears can flow freely, these tears are created in the eyesight of Love, I let them flow in peace... FREE.

Weeks have passed no sight of Sam. I find myself at the very spot we met, so many months ago. The spot where true love stained my soul. I am now sitting on the same rock that Sam did. I sit in the spirit of his kindness and patience, hoping I will get the same peace that was once extended to me. Heart thumping, maybe it was borrowed goods meant only for the moment, goods he needed back for the saving of his own soul... maybe... just maybe.

The breeze hits my face as the sun gives the last bit of hope I have, outside of the Dobbie I found in the bottom of my pants pocket. I don't know man, shit, I don't know about this life, bullshit too much for one man. A voice calls my name during what seems to be a moment of defeat, turn around and to my surprise there is Sam! We spend a few minutes talking about his life as he explains that his son is now going to school to Learn Brail.

Sam used a few choice words talking to his son about the importance of checking the direction of the wind before taking a pee. His patience warms the atmosphere, as he consistently coaches his sons' hand back toward the sharp hook, teaching him how to carefully check for the sharp point to successfully pierce the worm.

I ask him, how do you have the patience to raise a child that desperately requires all your attention. He responds, "Core Foundation, without this, I would have fell victim to the same dark voices of despair and defeat as my wife did." A Core Foundation, what's that? It's the only part of your life that is not subject to change, your responsibility is to feed it. He continues, the core foundation doesn't change like feelings, emotions and even people. I sat and thought about what he was saying, "it's like one minute you think someone is down for you, and ya'll good and then the next minute, they act like they don't even know you, and if I hear you right, everything in our lives fluctuates but this Core Foundation never changes its statement. Sam replies, yelp! It's the only reliable part of our lives, the inner source."

The feeling of being able to be anchored into a part of me I can rely on, are virgin words to my ears. I never heard of… shit I always relied on how I was currently feeling, and my emotions to guide my every move… mother fucka felt like doing something, I did it. I can be anchored in my Core Foundation, because it's not a chameleon as I am, as life can be, and as the vows to love and protect me turned out to be… like me.

I pondered more on the idea of building my own Core Foundation, a great distraction from the many thoughts racing in my mind, aligned with the warm light breeze kissing my face and swaying my dreads. The feeling I am expressing, is more relaxing than the bomb ass weed Big T smokes with me. Sam's reaction to the fish he caught, snapped me out of my daze, speaking rapidly, as if the question threatened to abandon me, I ask, "how do I began to develop my Core Foundation?" The smile on Sam's face spoke to me as if to say... welcome.

To begin building your Core Foundation, you must start by asking yourself questions like: What are my talents and abilities? what are my goals and dreams? I interrupted, "Man I'm telling you right now, every time I have ever wrote down my dreams and goals the shit takes me to a deep dark sad ass place, because the shit reminds me of what didn't happen! Putting my head down, my mama or daddy don't give a dam about... Sam stops me, your goals and dreams will always be who you are, I understand your living environment didn't support and help you grow these areas in your life. I know you had to put your goals and dreams on hold, making them no less of value, just a later time to activate and bring them to life."

Sam asked, "What brings light in your life," I'm not asking how bright the light is shining, I'm only asking what has light in your life. I reply, "being a father," my daughter creates so much of my light. I ain't been there for her, but I want to, I just... Sam steps in to say," if being a father brings light in your life, write it down, take one step at a time, don't rush the process.

Sam took his focus off our conversation to assist his son with preparing a sandwich. I am honored to bear witness to the patience a man holds for his child. The death and blind state of this child has not stolen away any of his ability to hear and see the goodness of Unconditional Love.

I asked, "What's your strongest Core quality?" Sam replied with great pride, Jesus! He is the Anchor to my Core. "Well, I could see why he would love you, taking such care of your special son and all." Not me, shit Jesus ain't worried about me, he doesn't even... Sam proclaimed, "Stop right their Knuckle Head, you're wrong," Jesus is not a chameleon, like people in our lives. I step in, "my mama and grandmama truth be told the preacher too, has told me all my life, until I do right, God ain't gone have nothing to do with me, so shit I feel like he spends his time with people doing right, going to school and shit like that, college stuff I guess, I don't know."

Sam gives off a slight chuckle as he wipes the crumbs from his son's face, and then kisses each cheek, another reminder of the tenderness between a son and his father.

Sam expresses, "Jesus is good all the time, his love for you is not subject to change. There are times I don't love Jesus the way I should, especially when I think about my wife. I get very angry and disappointed and don't want nothing to do with speaking to Jesus, but you see, the anchor that holds me tight to Jesus, is not fueled by the love I have for him, but through the love he has for me."

The conversation has walked along side of me ever since that day, the reaping's are now starting to settle in my heart. I have now come to terms with the importance of creating my Core Foundation. I am in dire need of a safe space for my mind to rest when all kinds of crazy breaks loose, I can't imagine forever being cocooned and wrapped in a protection, that doesn't flip flop on me, don't play games with me and it doesn't depend on how I feel about myself... falling to my knees savior.

Blind Trust is the only Trust I have ever known; this trust has fueled my mind and body compassing my life. Blind Trust, defined as my fuck ups, and my parents leaving me lonely and cold to these ugly dark streets. I unknowingly trusted I could live my life through this lens and eventually find happiness.

True Trust is starting to put cracks in the dark blanket covering my soul. True Trust is starting to fight its way in, through the power of Jesus, now I can see my light flickering on my strengths and life goals. I'm learning True Trust isn't about hitting the mark every day and, in every way, it's not about shaming myself, it's the knowledge of my Core, which is now the compass leading me tenderly with a constant forward nudge.

I am not perfect neither are my ways, however, my Core is my Foundation, my Source. The goal now is to feed it every day, its feels good knowing I am nourishing and placing time and attention into a source only having the ability to get stronger and serve my soul with an overflow of richness.

Sam explained, the first step in feeding your Core is giving appreciation to the opening of your eyes. The storms of life, carry heavy winds that weigh on your back, I do not fear, my fearless state does not exist through any human directed contributes... I'm starting to ride the waves anchored, supported with Truth eye wide open.

Big T was shot last night in the legs tryna keep that punk ass dude from hitting on his mama. His legs no longer support his body so the first of the month that once represented a time to get the "smokers" income, and stay flossed out in Jordan and Gold, has now been exchanged for the ugly reminder standing in the presence of being "dissed" by the homies because you can't make moves the ways he used to. Dis, by the females who don't see much value in someone in a wheelchair, dis by the woman you protected as her hands reach for first dibs on the check. Big T is second classman to his moms' heart as he watches the same man enter the home, that my bruh now pays to live in.

I'm just now able to write again, Son of Bitches wouldn't give me my dam shit out the hotel they kicked me out of couldn't pay the weekly rate. I tapped lightly on my grandmother's door slightly describing the unsureness lingering over me, not knowing if my taps will go unheard, unnoticed... the door opens, and my grandmothers' smile welcomes me in. I keep my clothes in my trash bag, because the dark-skinned man stretched out on the couch, is the reassurance my stay will be short lived. The food she cooks is so good, and the look in her face as she watches me devour it is priceless, along with the cigarette hanging out of her mouth I guess to give way to the hard work she performs in the kitchen... Go Grandma Go!

My Grandmother is asking me about my mom causing those hurtful feelings to take a seat with us at the table. I look up from my last bite of rice, and across the table the empty chair adjacent to me, looks like I can see the silhouette of my mother, hold on... only as child. I'm wondering why she is crying it appears to be tears going down her eyes. I look up from the sudden slam of the door, and it's my grandpa, my moms' father, she raises from her chair, running to the arms of her father, she stops suddenly, he disappears, dropping her head she looks back at her mom and runs out the room. The reflection of my grandmothers parenting helps me cut out a small art of love, from the construction of my heart, and I left it in the chair where my mom once sat, maybe one day she will find it. I replied to my grandmothers' questions with mostly, "I don't know" and lots of shoulder shrugs, safe responses, family responses... protected just for me responses.

Months went by with no sight of Sam at the Lake, however, my daily check in at the park has held perfect attendance. My daughter is growing, she is not close to a year old. Her little face and feet hide behind her mother when I wave at her. I'm looking deeper into the soul of Jazmin as she talks, examining her beautiful natural plump lips, and then I slowly use my eyes to address every curve she has and resting my eyes on her beautiful thighs, she interrupts my thoughts, "Excuse me, shit did you hear anything I just said?" I got you, I know what I need to do, can I climb through ya window tonight, like back in the day, "Boy, please!" She may be built with a little attitude and sassy at times, her backbone withstands the army of pressures in the world, Black Woman, I don't want to forget to mention, been too busy. Thank You truly for holding down our race of people.

The bright sun begins to dawn on my Tuesday, grateful for the light it's still willing to share. I am walking around the Car Wash, when I notice hanging out of the dumpster a few shirts and nice pair of jeans. Securing my left arm around my findings, I hear a deep voice and long story short, this is where I met Dexter the manager of the Car Wash. I got the job! Over lunch one day Dexter talked to me about all the times he watched me get stuff out the dumpster, he continued to talk about how he couldn't understand, what might have been going on in life. I will always remember the words he spoke when he said, "looking out at you scrabbling around in the dumpster I thought, what has happened in this man's life were digging in dumpsters has taking the place of self-responsibility."

The words, laughter and conversations that grew in our friendship would be one of the biggest breaking points to the fuel lighting my fire to live and grow. He started talking to me, and I started listening. I'm understanding more on how I have been living and surviving on my list of "Lack", parts of my life I was dealt, things I was too young to carry, burdens breaking the backs of children.

I innocently awarded the word Survival with a Position of Power rooted in Lack, not knowing the impact in the roots of its existence. Survival is a word of stagnation when rooted in your "Lacks". Survival is a growing divine when rooted from your strengths. Lack is the defeating map of ones' survival it says, "this is all the shit I was lacking; my survival is getting clothes out the dumpster, selling dope other peoples might be robbing and killing... just a Boy/Man trying to live from his Lacks... he doesn't know...Teach him... Lost Child."

Waking up repeating the same actions with that "I don't give a Fuck" mentality, caught in the strong web of giving my energy and attention into feeding the "Lacks" ... Stuck.

True Survival is shaped by the constant reflection on the characteristics and qualities one possess that make you Proud of Who you Are, ask yourself this question, "What are the qualities you can share with another person? knowing these qualities will help grow a good friendship?" answering these questions make up the authentic resilient root existence to survival.

The days swiftly pass, thinking about my baby girl, she will be turning one soon. My anger remains at a Premature stage, flipping out and shit at work at times, throwing shit a little harder than usual and smacking my lips in combination with the "Whatever Man" attitude. I know the anger I feel toward my mama and daddy, all that Pain be still fucking with me, I see my change in life, I ain't denying that at all... Gotta get this shit up out of me, hurts man... lingering.

Dexter took me to get lunch, the look on his face indicated to me he had a need to speak. Pulling up at the Lake is perfect for me because I am blanketed by the environment that cradles my anxious feelings to the unknown words he will spill. His words stuck to me as if what he said was a High School graduation speech I rehearsed to the audience of my heart.

Dexter expressed, "Knuckle Head I see your anger and to be real my anger comes from my parents too." My parent struggle doesn't derive from places like not being around or not providing basic needs type shit but placed so much of their opinions and thoughts on how "I should be," that we created a shared abandonment of the "Who I was meant to be?" I'll never forget it, listening next the door as my parents talked about me. I remember discovering for the first time the evaluation of my Worth in the eyes of my mom and dad. In a very disappointing tone, my father tells my mother, "The boy will not be a doctor, and I will not shame this family or the achievers we strive to maintain, decision has been made to give him a disability. I will place a phone call to my psychiatrist, good friends will make sure he finds that disability. I want to feel safe when asked why he has falling so far from the tree." A tear raced down Dexter's face, "man you call your son disabled to do what." The shield to comfort the curse.

I respectfully moved only my eyes toward Dexter, watching the tears flush his face. I will not interrupt his flow; I know one quick shift in my body could lead to an interference or sudden stop in such an intimate/vulnerable moment. I waited till all his feelings were able to return home, before asking the question, "Why you still cry, if you say you respect it and got control over it?" Taking a deep breath he replied, "I do got it under control, hold up, nah let me rephrase that, I have a Healthy Frame of Reference not control a difference." I wrinkle my nose up, head cocked back, "what you talking about bruh?" He looked at me not saying a word and only his eyes moved to the notebook laying on his truck dashboard. According to Dexter a Healthy Frame of Reference will cloth me with understanding, so I am no longer responding to the situation with shook up, scared, naked, and broke emotion.

The purpose of the Healthy Frame of Reference is to now rely on an understanding of everything that is attached to the situation. The Frame of Reference is where your mind will move to any time you get to thinking or replaying shit in ya head, the Frame of Reference teaches you how to respect the hard emotions and feelings that will always be married to the situation, but don't have to be in the place of power when the memory shows up in the mind. Respect and Power two different words. Respecting your past is giving clarity that you can't change the feelings that come with the situation, so why do we Respect feelings? So, you free yourself from being a Prisoner to those feelings.

The cycle of diving into and pouring your current energy into those negative feelings that will always be attached to that situation will stunt the growth meant to happen from the situation.

The Respectful Bowl helps you change your statement about how you verbally express the situation, before creating the Respectful Bowl the word "Still" is addressed. One must start off practicing the removal of the word "Still" when verbalizing the situation. For example, "I'm still mad at mama and daddy, they got me fucked up, treated me like this!" A statement like this reflects on the word "Still", which gives an understanding that this person's feelings about how his parents treated him is still in a place of power when he speaks on how he feels about his parents. Meaning his negative feelings are still controlling the situation... still a prisoner to it. Here is an example of a person that has given their feelings and emotions Respect but not Power in reference to an experience. "There will always be feelings of anger, it was fucked up the way they treated me. However, I had not control over how they treated me, but I will not allow how I feel about how they treated me to keep me in a place of imprisonment I want to continue to grow from this experience. Notice, this person did not deny their feelings, they didn't try to erase what they feel for that situation, but they didn't use the word "Still" to represent that their new energy was being placed into those defeating emotions.

The first step is called the Respectful Bowl. In this step you will clarify the situation in good detail not leaving out any parts of the situation you know you still dig right into those negative feelings any minute you are reminded of the situation. Next to each one of the experiences write down all those negative feelings that are attached to each specific situation this step is important to give clarity that you have not bottled up any feelings that you feel toward the situation.

Trips to the lake are always so fulfilling, giving me an opportunity to free my mind from that bull-shittin' job. I'm thankful for the job, I guess what I am saying is that people come in and get the car washed by a black man and automatically assume I ain't shit or that's as far as I'm going to go in life. I am telling you this because today these little "think them somethin'" females rolling their eyes and smacking their lips demanding what they want done to their car had me heated, my unimproved self would have said, F this job I'm out, and then walked out being pissed about the way they behaved toward me combined with the assumptions created in my head about how they felt about who I am as a person.

I don't need you to explain common sense ways to conduct myself in your car.

I feel less than a human in this moment as I enter the vehicle, she must really think there was no possible way I could have ever learned how to conduct myself in car. She rushes toward me, I can see her in the left side mirror, my heart starts thumping, what the hell going on, I ain't touched nothing in this woman car, real talk I just sat down. She rushes her car, can you please get out for just one second, she climbs in to grab the change out of her console, combined with that fake ass side smile. Times like this would have usually led me to a place of repeat... back to the streets carrying around the crippling words "I tried that work shit, and it ain't for me."

I was able to reflect on my Core Foundation and hear the words of Sam talking to me. I remember him talking about being in the moments of defeating feelings and self-worth conflict, but to bypass those thoughts instead ruminate and dwell in the Love Jesus has for me along with the characteristics and qualities he knows Makes Me One Amazing Person, and how Jesus gives you the Strength to Nourish these aspects. And in this moment I ask My Jesus walk with me now, and in this moment I'm rushed with warm intense feelings covering every organ in my body... I take a deep breath, close my eyes and what blows my mind, is that I realized my mindset was placed on repeat as I watched myself jump into the pool of who Jesus says I am, constant mental attention into the picture of my jump into his grace... if you don't mind... one more jump... before closing your pages.

Jesus has given me access to his Power, through my reflection of the Love he has for me, I can then Nourish these areas of Who I am? through this Powerful cycle I was able to withstand the passing of my storm. I couldn't have changed that women's attitude about me prior to her meeting me or even in the moment of us getting acquainted. I noticed how good I felt cleaning her tires and vacuuming her car. I realize every motion I made was for the purpose of nourishing my characteristics, operating out of the understanding for the Love Jesus has for me, not trying to operate out of the Love I have for myself.

Jesus holds the only Love Statement on your life, never subject to change.

Dexter let me know lunch was on him again, I was happy about that, he talking about a brother been doing good at work, I appreciate the compliment. I feel like I'm starting to learn the true definition of a Leader. I can hear Dexter right now saying "if you don't yet know how to stand last in line and still represent your Leadership skills, then when in Power one will be drenched in their insecurities, ignited by ignorance, then set a fire, all entertained by your closest friends."

Lunch was great Dexter and I enriching our friendship over lunch and good conversation. The Red notebook still lingering on his dashboard got my attention. Dexter picked up our conversation from our last lunch break. "Remember the Healthy Frame of Reference I was talking to you about?" I respond.

"I hope I never forget it!" He began, the second step in developing your Frame of Reference is called the "Learning Aspect." There are two questions you must answer in this step.

1. What negative things did you Learn and now practice, behaviors, or actions that been done unto you that you now do to others. I learned from what I experienced growing up to treat females like they weren't worth much, always feeling insecure therefore assuming that she was comparing me to other men, quickly defensive, all this heavy weight keeps me on edge. The constant suffocating cycle of shaming and blaming, rehearsing my childhood, downplaying my potential along with a cloud walking around my head saying, "I don't think I got what it takes," is the attitude weighing down my forward steps. The mixture of emotions and negative thinking keeps me in a

place of envy, words like, "they got it, they should have it."

Dexter replies, talking cash money shit when people come around is cool sometimes, I'm realizing a lot of that comes from pain, sinking down a little in his truck," just thinking man, I used to look at what my friends were wearing or just anybody I was around and like I always had something to say, fucking up the mood, people would laugh, but it still put a negative ass vibe in the room… real talk. I commented, I'm more of a fist fighter, working on it now, but man it's like whatever happened to me, I want to be able to give that pain back out, anything doesn't go my way, you will feel my raft.

I was able to talk to him in greater detail about my childhood as lunch was wounding down. He was able to return to our conversation, due to the Semi-Truck pulling in requiring two men to wash and spray. He continued, "the seeds that didn't get the opportunity to grow like patients and communication." I started laughing, "communication" this man. Dexter explained, "the day parents take up the motto children should be seen and not heard, is the same day a grave will be dug for the upcoming funeral in the death of a parent/child's unconditional love. Chiming in, "I'm your parent not your friend," sounds familiar." Dereck expresses, when I heard my parents speak this way, I thought to myself, well if you're not my friend I guess me coming to you about my imperfections and my flaws isn't in your department to assist with, so I guess my parents are here just to police what I do, shout when I'm wrong, use that index finger to point out my mistakes, tell others how embarrassed they are of our flaws, acting just as an officer, serves us our list of faults, hopping back on their pedestal, speeding off from a heart break.

Sid came by to talk to me about Little Marshall. Sid expressed, "they got my brother in the county, got him pinned up on some bull-shit charges." I replied, "tell him to hit me up when he touchdown." "Sid sho is fine, I wouldn't even try it, that's my homie sister, plus I would hate to have to beat up her little boyfriend."

The sun regained its position up against my brown skin, as the sweat rolled down my forehead. Dexter waves his hand toward me an indication it's time to take a break. The cold air welcomes me when I enter the break, Dexter tosses me a bottled water and a bag of chips. He sits down and picks right back up as if he never stopped talking, "Step 3 is developing your Healthy Frame of Reference," I scrabble for paper, ripping the last two sheets from a log in folder. He continues, "this is the Action Stage, where you reflect on your day-to-day growth from the situation." I start thinking about how I treat women and I know that part of my Frame of Reference is to listen more, work not being so quick to get offended about my mess ups, because I can change.

I understand that I am never solely defined by any one mess up in my life, so I don't constantly find myself trying to live and operate change out of a Prison. Dexter committed, "I got two kids by two different women, rolling his eyes, "you know how that go," with my kids they know I love um and I am both parent and friend.

My children know my mistakes and I'm not Perfect. I try to make sure I'm not so quick to say "hush, I don't wanna hear it." Another area I try to remind them is that people's opinion about our relationship will never be the driven force in the evaluation of the strength we hold for each other. The number one thing I make sure I am teaching is that Jesus is the only Love that you can solely depend on to stand up in during your toughest times. Lighting a cigarette, he continues, "I tell them the love I have for can stand the test of time, I love you to the moon and back, but the love Jesus has for you will out reign even my ability to love you." Sitting in this moment, I feel goosebumps on my arm surfacing around my neck and up my spine.

I am starting to understand how to build my frame of reference, so when I am starting to think about my past and how my parents treated me, I know I must place my mind into the statement, "how I am growing every day, and in what ways." Placing new energy and attention into those past attached negative feelings will only lead into giving those past feelings power over my present moment. I can't afford continuing to be a prisoner to my pain. Moving forward in my life, whenever I am faced with situations happening in my life. I know the importance of using my three steps, so I can develop my Healthy Frame of Reference providing me a healthy inner conversation for when I am triggered and re-experiencing that situation.

I have been spending so much time talking with you. I know that you have always been needed in my life, a place to share and write my thoughts. I know I need to be around my homies, plus I ain't been around no cuties in a cool minute, another motivation to go out tonight, I got tomorrow off, let's get it!

I know it has been a few days since I have had time to write. I figured you would be interested in find out how things went hanging with the fellas. Big T yells, "Why da fuck is dude sitting on the arm of my couch!" I turned to see Little Marshall, he posted up like he didn't know da rules, he replied, "my fault" moving quickly to the couch.

Usually, Little Marshall got some silly shit to talk about... but today was different. He asked me a question, deeper than I have ever gone with him or even given his brain credit for the possibility of being capable of exploring. He said, "Knuckle Head you think I act like a kid?" I gave him that look like, do you really wanna go there, he looked at me and started laughing. "I'm asking you because I ran into a few home girls of mine and we were sitting around talking and they were all like, I take life in as a child.

Big T shouted from the kitchen, "you do, look how many times I dun had to tell ya butt to stay off the arm of my couch and you keep doing that stuff." Little Marshall rolled his eyes, anyway, Deidra been knowing me since we were about eight years old and she said that I am always trying to shine through my faults, whatever that's supposed to mean."

I waited a moment inhaling the last puff of the blunt before my thumb became a victim.

I started my conversation with Little Marshall first letting him know the good that I see in him, the qualities that he brings into our friendship it means a lot to someone when you can first fill them in on their positive so they can walk into their struggles with strength not deflation. I continued, "I love you bruh, think about this, the next time you meet up with Deidra you show her apart of you that you are Proud of," the look on his face is priceless. "Proud of," falling back into the couch like he had just been shot by a twelve gages. Big T walked in the room, interrupting the passionate moment that even Little Marshall couldn't resist. Handing him twenty bucks, "take this, think about what you love, what you are proud of, don't play yourself by focusing on an "image" as your starter guide in being proud of you, think about standing alone in this world and writing the love of you on the biggest chalkboard with no humans to utter a word, shining through why you love you." Little Marshall smiles at me, a smile I've never seen before. I'm now writing about this memory, I always giggle because as soon as he cracked that smile, hopped off the couch, headed to the kitchen and right before leaving out he turned back to say, "that is a better way to get to Deidra and that booty," laughing walking out the door.

    The beer I split last night has caused a spot in one of your pages, I apologize for that, I will not be ripping any pages from you and replacing it with a new, would only be a testimony of an unwilling part of me to accept your imperfections a side of you that has been so gracious toward me. Moments of pain still pound heavy in my chest, like a synchronized group of Cheyenne Indians drumming fiercely as they drive away the people of advantage. Haven't heard from my mom in about, well a while, noting the months will only pin down the pain, not allowing a kick of survival to highlight the moment. Baby sister keeps me updated about mama, as she waves her hands with attitude as she expresses her thoughts about our mom. Talking about how she has met a younger guy and housing him and some more... I left the conversation learning a valuable lesson, a lesson I hold in secret to you. I would like to share with others but announcing this statement to anybody would relinquish the right to their opinion. I would be debating rules to agree to disagree and in return be declared a rebel. I stand for the motto: "don't put up with bull-shit from a person in a relationship that you claim you couldn't bare putting up with in your own child."

The sand pushing through my feet steals the attention. I usually have set for the warmth of the sun that kisses my cheeks beaming down on my greased forehead.

I'm here for responsibility today, I want to apologize early so you don't get your hopes up for your usual. I am aware of the expectation of getting the nourishment you so desperately need. I know I fill you with so much of my burdening moments. I'm not being neglectful, but the moment you are depending on will have to take second place today. The Peace I receive here is entangled with the swelling anger toward my parents.

Routine visits to the Lake have made me aware of a jealously I face, knowing that with the chains broken from the unbearable feelings placed in my heart around my parents, there will be a missing space to be filled... with somebody.

Developing a Healthy Frame of Reference is a must. I, truly, know now that I need a mental reference that I can go to. So, when what they did come to mind, I got a reference I can lean into, helping me move out of that moment without the automatic feelings of wanting to knock a motherfucka out that look wrong.

Respectful Bowl

Mom – always thinking about her and what she needed. I dislike these phrases so dam much, phrases like, "I gotta life too," this always makes me angry, because right after that she would always attach a selfish ass act to it, "yall go in the room company here." Her famous lines seem to come with different periods of my life. Her famous line," Boy you need to get ya shit together," was between the ages of sixteen-eighteen years of age. The phrase, "What da hell wrong with you?" was between the ages of fifteen-thirteen. Ages eleven-thirteen "I know you don't call ya self being mad, you outa be happy somebody takin' care of your ass. The ages seven-ten the phrase, circled around." Don't embarrass me, I don't got time for no bullshit, not today." Seven years old and younger was mostly spent arguing with my dad giving more attention to his bullshit and what he was doing instead of using that attention on me.

Tears are slowing streaming down my face; I will not run my tears holds a major represented as the Presenter to the party of my life.

My Dad – always saying what he has done and never did it, constant disappointment.

He never seemed to have the confidence to stand on his own, the little time we did spend together was usually him introducing me to another female and a new couch.

The feelings that will always be attached are anger,

disappointment, feeling like I wasn't worth much, not feeling wanted, feelings like I don't belong.

I am now learning the importance of placing respect on these feelings not to give them power. Negative feelings are part of the story true enough they just don't get the leading role. The more I seen the more I adopted, if my parents' treatment toward me was formed into a trophy I would be standing there dressed in an all-black tuxedo, ready to receive it, every negative statement, name calling phrase used against me, creates the blueprint of how I talk to the inner me.

I notice it's hard for me to define my self-worth without the combination of shaming and blaming. Things will go wrong for me and I either say, "Just how shit is what y'all expect" or people think they better then you, I'm gonna show you something watch this!" I now see how my self-worth has always been a chameleon always changing, just really based off what has happened in the day. I don't want to miss out on talking about the influence of how trying to get outside acceptance acts as an aid in the suffering of myself worth.

I need my homies to think, I mean know that I am that "one." I depend on cheers and high fives and when they are not loud enough for my satisfaction, I go to great lengths to make sure my hunger for approval gets met. Starting fights, running up and socker punching people, randomly disrespecting people I don't even know and even asking my homies what wild shit they wanted to see me do.

Watching my father go from place to place and never having the confidence to have a place of his own and supporting his actions with the famous statement, "at least you got some where to stay," came so naturally that by the time I was nine years of age, he had convinced me that God didn't grant him access to take care of himself. I protected him with my ignorance, protection from the names people called him such as "bum ass dude," an ignorance shielding him from having the responsibility of answering the questions. I want to demand answers from questions wrapped around the love I couldn't grow from me to him.

I need to walk away from the process for just a minute, letting my eyes drift off entertained by the frogs lying flat on the rocks daring to be bothered. I dip my toes in and out of the water as I listen to the bird's chirp music of loyalty, puffing on my joint relaxed... staying grateful to what no man can replica... the lake.

I am not ready to dive back into this process of developing my frame of reference it feels good to be getting all this off my chest. I will have to take a step-in building trust for the love I want to have for myself, so recognizing how important it is for me to return and complete the development of my frame of reference along with giving myself time to process everything, then showing strength to return, will be the first strong evidence of being on the right path...True Trust.

The past few years all I have heard from others is, tell me your story, how did it impact you, that must have been difficult to deal with. Repetitive replies as such keep me dwelling and rehearsing in the past, love my therapist, maybe she didn't know... talk soon. The sun keeps nudging for the attention it deserves from me... closing my eyes.

Jasmine came by only after blowing her phone up so I

could see my daughter. The warmth of my daughters' little arms squeezing my neck is the safest place a man can be. I pledge to my daughter there will always be a fight in daddy's heart to always keep the U and the S together, nothing that anybody will ever say about you, can change the temperature of the unconditional love I have set for you. I will never evaluate your worth through the eyes of the outside world. Daddy understands that my anger toward my past, can't guide my decisions in life, if I don't want to jeopardize the U and the S in our love.

Providing for you is not a feelings-based role in my life. When it's time to hit that J.O.B. I can't allow my feelings to fuel my decision on rather or not to show up at my job. I want to make sure you can attend school with no worries is my responsibility. I want to stand proud in your eyes not just mine. I want you to reap value through the actions I hold for maintaining love between us. Love is more than the eyes that meet the face of the loved one. My eyes may fall weak at times with my shaken circumstances, so I declare our love baby girl in the eyes of Jesus, it is only now that I can stand boldly in saying the U and the S can withstand any test at any time... Love Dad.

Had to come and let ya know ya boy got a raise! I feel good I got the raise, the homie was laughing, talking about dam you happy for a funky ass fifty percent raise, I took a deep breath smiling and replied "yelp" the reason for the raise is more important than the dollar amount. The raise lets me know as a person I'm making personal growth; fuck the amount I'll worry about that later.

I'm Learning more and more that true inner growth is never conquered by mastering the mechanics of the outer me. To accept the idea that one can build true long-lasting self-worth from the outer you, would also be found guilty with no need of trial, to the acceptance of living by the motto, of making your outer parts responsible for the inner you. There can never be a relinquish to the responsibility of the inner you in defining your self-worth, and if you remain guilty to this said warning, you will forever remain a stubborn pre-school child, trying to force a square block in a circle shaped container... frustrated!

I'm sitting at Big T's house along with Jazmin, you know the days where the rain has left its mark of wet porches and muddy footprints is the description, I give this moment. Jazmin's extra self-had to start talking about a brother's toes. I'm laughing while writing; I been on her though; I know you ain't talking with ya no booty having self, rolling her eyes and flirty pushes is her response. Jazmin looked at Big T and blurted words I've been to be intimated to ask or say, not due to fear of how he would respond, but that his response may act as a piece of saran wrap, keeping his pain from deteriorating.

Jazmin continued "You gotta girlfriend, I don't ever see you talking to anybody and not much on ya social media, what's up with that?" Big T shifted in his wheelchair as if he needed to get prepared to answer the question. "Nah, not really," he replied. "I haven't really been nowhere or do shit really cause of this, as he looks down at his wheelchair." I jumped up diving right into the conversation, "You can't say I don't be asking you to go with me," first thing you say is, "Nah, man, I'm good."

I felt good letting my feelings out to my best friend. "Bruh I want to let you know it's never any problem with me helping you." Big T interrupted, "I know man... I know you, I interrupted, No I want you to know that nothing chances with us... man nothing." Big T, replies, "Dude I know, where is all this coming from?" I reply, "Trying to get you to escape off this front porch with me." I continued, "There is a party on Friday, can I come get you, will my boy come hang with a playa!" Big T replied, "yes only thing is to be honest every time I pick my clothes out, get dressed, these negative thoughts come flooding in, as if commanded to evade, conquer and take hostage of my self- confidence."

Jazmin hops back in, "you are rehearsing in their thoughts." Big T, exclaimed.

"Rehearsing?" As he was looking Jazmin all upside her head, "where you get that word."

Jazmin continued, "I'm just saying in the moment the reason why your confidence is being drained is the amount of time you place feeding into those flooding thoughts, instead of placing respect on those feelings." I'm beginning to think, "where is this coming from?" Jazmin rose from her chair at the same time the thunder decided to strike, as if to tell Jazmin, I too want to be loved in this moment, and perhaps love is being answered, because as the rain pours, it seems to breast feed the thunderous roars right into a good night's rest.

Jazmin continues, "You know I had my baby at sixteen. I was so embarrassed, like at first, I was cool going to school, because I wasn't showing, but as time went on my most dreadful moment came." Jazmin continues, "I find myself six months pregnant, racing to make it to my next class escaping the rush of the hallways. Today, I do not master my skill, caught in the hallway trying to navigate through a football and cheerleading squad. Time has stopped, and every eye has fell on examining my body, from the bottom of my feet to the top of my head and then vacation at my mid-section."

Jazmin sits back down exhaling a deep breath as if the intensity of the message carries so much weight. Like she was trying to embrace herself for the flood of emotions rushing her body. She goes on to talk about how she met this nurse during her pregnancy, and she grew a bond and how the nurse taught her how to practice a four-step mental process that has helped her not feed into negative thoughts. Jazmin continued talking, "I'm not good enough, and shits over now," Are my defeating thoughts that always try to suffocate my confidence. I listen in more as Jazmin is speaking and she describes these negative statements as words that had her constantly losing sight of her qualities, as if her qualities had somehow disappeared now that she was mother.

The first step is recognizing the presence of the negative thought (s), don't ever feel like negative thoughts don't need to be addressed when they present in the mind, denying and not addressing is dangerous, "waiting to deal" with negative thoughts leaves a lot of space for those thoughts to gain authority over your thought thinking the rest of the day, in other words every decision that you make will reflect from that negative pattern of thinking the rest of the day and in most cases the rest of our lives.

Big T jumped up with excitement as if every word that Jazmin said pumped another breath of air in his lifeless body. "I'm starting to get what you're saying make sense, it be like when I hear people say, I'm going to distract myself into my job or my career and deal with shit later, as if those thoughts at some point in the day are going to respect who you are, show you compassion and lighten the burden. To only realize that those dismissed thoughts now demand attention that will sit with you at your family dinner table, speak through your communication with your partner and children, slowly chipping away at your self-worth." I'm so grateful in this moment that I have you to write to, I am so proud I didn't think he had it in him to speak out like that, adding on to the reason he is my best friend.

Jazmin's powerful presentation in this moment rightfully stole my attention as she continued. "The second step is Respecting negative thoughts not to give them Power." Respecting negative thinking keeps it from moving into a place of Power. Respecting negative thinking means you acknowledge these are the thoughts, taking a deep breath and sitting with the thoughts. The step teaches you the importance of not bottling up or suppressing those uneasy thoughts, trying to use these tactics will automatically move those thoughts into a place of Power.

The third step is capturing the negative thought. This is such an important step... simply put it can't be looked over. I'm looking at my baby mama she so sassy, I love this girl." Regaining her standing position, Jazmin continues her declaration to the world. Capturing the negative thought says freezing those thoughts, placing a net around the thoughts. Capturing negative thinking means you are staying in that moment of thinking; you are not dwelling in the past looking back at similar spaces in time where you felt this way nor are you rehearsing into assumptions about your future worries regarding negative future thinking.

Jazmin would go on to talk about how most people don't realize what makes a negative thought so Powerful and it's not the initial thought itself, it's the weight it carries after the "feeding."

I hoped up so quick, "Dang Dude your dog just shook all over me and now my dam notebook is wet, just one page though. Big T grabbed his dog's chain and commanded his ass to sit, I responded "okay cool, thank you." Jazmin sided with me, "Yes sir I would hate to have to declare war between me and your dog, over a splash of mud on my new kicks," she turned toward me gave me a wink and a smile, "I'm just saying, I laugh to myself as I silently announce to only you, her head is big enough, but she so Fire!"

The rain is beginning to slow down, and I'm itching to find out what step four is about as I watch anxiously as Jazmin finishes up her last bite of sandwich. The fourth step is replacing the negative thought with a healthier pattern of thinking, so you can move through that moment. There are two actions that take place in the replacement process of thinking. The first action response is titled "My Speak Back." A Speak Back is defined as the healthy pattern of thinking that derives from your Core Foundation. To have as strong dependent reliable "Speak Back," one must be determined daily to nourish their Core Foundation. Big T, cuts in the conversation, "why do I need to spend time strengthening my Core Foundation if I know it already?" Jazmine replied, "if you are not waking up every morning with an adopted mindset that there is an obligation and responsibility to pour into the very areas in your life that you will be depending on, then what will continue to happen is that your Core Foundation will remain weak therefore hindering your ability, motivation and trust, in creating healthy Speak Backs."

The words Core Foundation floated in the air as if to have grabbed and taking all three of us hostage. Core Foundations is being treated in the same way we treat Funeral attire, it's in the closet its important, you know you'll need it one day, but the only time its useful is during a tragedy. The only difference the funeral attire can display its presence on the flesh while the Core foundation remains a simple undergarment during a negative experience... not even to be seen.

The snap of Jazmin's fingers placed me back in the conversation. The second action step is the Behavioral Response. In this step she goes on to explain that the Behavioral Response is the added supportive action to your Speak Back. The Behavioral Response acts as the extra validation you place action into moving out of the negative thought or moment. The first way to start working on Strengthening a healthy behavioral response is physically getting up and moving from that initial spot where you experienced that negative thought. Big T, chimed in, "I know I can read a disrespectful message or text, and really be stuck physically in that moment."

The Behavioral response is termed the extra validation because it is not responsible in leading you through a negative pattern of thinking. Relying solely on the behavioral response to lead you through an uneasy moment, leads you into a practice of distracting yourself from your thoughts, rather than moving through your thoughts, encouraging you to develop a believe system that the Speak Back no longer needs to stand in the first response position.

When this happens the behavioral response switches roles going from assisting in the moment into being held responsible for the entirety, leaving the behavioral response overwhelmed and defeated from the daily beatings it receives through self-hatred statements as you become the prime witness to the decline in your desire to love what you love living for.

Jazmin explains, "Miss Fondro is a lady I will never forget she put me up on a lot of game and for that I will always be grateful." Big T what does your four steps look like. I looked up immediately being the first one to capture the look on his face. He replied, "I don't know," motioning for his dog to lay on his lap. He continues Step.

1: Recognizing the thought, immediately when you were talking about that I started thinking about my weight. Every sense I been in a wheelchair I just been spending a lot of my time on my phone, watching T.V. and eating. I realize the minute I start even thinking about making a change I'm already met with negative words like, you have tried this before, let it go, love me for who I am or F- you.

I'm understanding now I am not to beat myself up, but accept that these are my present thoughts, this step is like the action switch to the process. Accepting my thoughts positions my mental to start working on the moving through cycle rather than to spend time frustrated and pissed that I'm having the thoughts which then allows those negative emotions to act as a distraction and I lose sight of the importance of regulating finding myself camping out in those negative moments.

"I love me, and I want to start making some small changes, yes, I have these negative thoughts that's going to try in distract me, I will not battle them. First off when you said Respect vs Power, I was thinking they meant the same thing, and then when you got to talking, I said OK that's been my problem, every time thoughts about my weight come to mind, I been given them power, moving forward in what I have heard you say, respecting negative thinking keeps them from moving into a place of power."

The response I have for step 2: I can respect I'm having these negative feelings and thoughts popping up every time I'm in the process of thinking about losing weight and getting back healthy. Big T appears to be very excited to talk, I even feel better when I use the word Respect when addressing negative thinking. Big T nods his head as if he just made an agreement with his confidence and self-worth.

I really must work on capturing negative thinking. I find myself dwelling in the past or just losing motivation in the moment, because of all the assumptions I'm placing in my head about my future, but if I start practicing what you are saying and began throwing a net over what I'm thinking in the moment, meaning I capture not feed negative thinking to be in a position of replacement.

I find myself more and more blaming God and putting a wall of resentment between the conversation that he wants to have with me. I know my resentment is rooted in the questions, why you let me be the one to get shot and look at me in this damn wheelchair. I start comparing myself to all my homeboys, what they can do? What chicks they can pull all this Pressure Thinking leads me to feeling defeated and stuck right in the F Zone. F this and F that ready to just lay someone down at any time, just mad you know… hurt it's like I have grabbed on to that pain and have been protecting it ever since.

The weight I have gained all my failed attempts to lose the weight combined with all the days and nights I remember sitting up in bed, watching my weight increase and acting as if I don't care, will always be attached to frustrating and disappointing feelings and emotions. I've always thought I had to battle negative thinking while trying to stay committed to a health plan. Looking at it now, I have been trying to shame and blame myself into progress.

The most vital step in my journey in getting healthy will be to feed my Core Foundation the first thirty days. Remembering the Core is broken down into two parts. Jesus' definition of who I am to him combined with the positive qualities and aspects I want to execute in this world. The journey to getting my body healthy, I know is going to come with some waves and a lot of Unknowns. I'm facing this area in my life equipped with the Known therefore my mind will be quick to reference the definition of who I am in Jesus who says I'm able and protected.

I feel so FREE knowing I'm not facing my weight issue depending on my individual strength, I know I'm only human and there will be times along the way, I fall short of my goals and strides and trying to reflect on the definition I hold for myself in that moment is tainted and of little use. The definition I hold for myself is subject to change, for example today I could be on cloud ten about my progress on eating a consistent healthy breakfast, but by the time dinner rolls around I could be cycling back into a spin of shaming and blaming myself, pressing the replay button to my misery.

The definition of who I am in the name of Jesus is not

subject to change. My actions or power will never be strong enough to change his definition of who I am and what I mean to him. The high-powered emotions I have can't destroy his love for me, no mistakes I make can change his definition of me, and I don't even have to earn it. I know when I reflect on the definition, I give myself it's usually defined by how I'm feeling, what the day brought me, who pissed me off or what dumb ass mistake I made, nor sir, I'm cool on allowing the definition I have for myself lead the way, I need something consistent, fearless, and definitely not subject to change.

Jazmin looked over at Big T with her glowing smile. The sun began to show its presence causing my eyes to squint along with sweat starting to run down the back of my neck. I'm in a trance, for the words I have witnessed calls my attention for my intentions... I can't deny.

Jazmin explained to operate out of an impactful Core Foundation, one must pour daily nourishment into it. The acceptance of allowing my Core Foundation to lead my everyday living, produces a consistent statement, when I awake each morning. The statement it produces says. "I am responsible for feeding my Core Foundation." The Core Foundation declaration paves away for adjustment to take place in the mindset when facing the day.

The mindset is altered in two ways. The inner conversation that is held when mistakes are made or when they are brought to me. The second alteration is the outside verbal response to the situation or circumstance. The inner conversation with mistakes or mishaps must be intertwined with one statement and that says, "how can I learn so I can grow from this situation." Practice training the mind. The statement must be applied to every situation accidently or intentional.

Deciding to only apply the statement "how can I learn so I can grow from this situation toward mistakes leaves the actions you will do with intent abandoned to shame and guilt and those words build a prison wall around that situation. The intentional situation sits behind those walls and drowns into those shaming and blaming feelings and emotions, leaving me with an attitude of "I did it, I fucked up, what's the point, might as well keep fucking up." I must grow from each situation in my life. Developing this understanding keeps my thoughts surrounded with the alignment of learning not in the development of creating a prison wall.

The second part of the mindset change is recognizing how much one invests in the outer dynamic of the experience. Investing into the experience is a reflection on how one defines it and how much one provides it. Be careful not to invest a definition of Power over the moment. Stay away from ending statements such as, "just one of those days," "there goes my day," "expected the worse go figure." These statements grant access for the moment to walk in a place of dominance. Healthy investment statements say, "one of these moments," every second left in a 24-hour day stands for an opportunity for change, "this morning wasn't the best however, there is still time in my day to leave a positive stain."

Jazmin started giggling a little as she continued, "I'm still working on not giving my moment more attention than it needs, a lot of the times I open too many opportunities to provide growth defined as prompting the problem. Actions like texting, posting on social media, sharing it with co-workers and going home after work making it the last conversation you have before going to bed all can be prompting the problem. Confining in others is very important, having the opportunity to release those feelings in the presents of the people you love can't be left unsaid, but even these conversations are done in a more intimate private manner.

Big T announces, "The journey I'm on to lose weight and get healthy has a Past, Present and Future. The understanding and acceptance of the past nights of overeating shaming and blaming, starting, and dropping plans to get healthier will always be attached to the feelings of anger, frustration, and disappointments, however, I can't allow my past along with these feelings lead the way in my Present. Today I will start my journey by committing my first thirty days into strengthening the Love in the belief I have for the definition of how Jesus Loves me unconditionally how it can't be moved, not even by me.

"I will write Jesus' Love for me down on paper, three times a day morning, noon, and night. I don't know exactly how my plan will be shaped or what equipment I will use or what building I will be in, but I'm no longer afraid to step off track on my journey. I will be equipped with being able to hold an encouraging conversation with my mishaps, mistakes, or short comings, realizing this helps me respect that every second in my day can be acknowledged by showing love toward my health. For example, if I didn't eat as well as I wanted in the morning, I will not promote that morning experience, I will define it implement the word

However, into my inner conversation granting me space to look forward into the rest of my hours holding my day, and continue to strive for another moment to reflect on the love I have for my body.

"When I meet people, I am also going to be working on no longer focusing on all the what ifs. What ifs are self-doubt, self- pity, anxiety, and stress. I want to respond to people from the qualities I hold in my self – worth." Big T looks at me, "I'll be ready Friday for the party… straight up."

The beat of the lonely heart thumping in my chest keeps sending broken signals. Missing its mark to fulfill the soul. I find myself here kneeling at the very steps of cruelty, looking up, eyes full of dripping hollow. The party will go on now, neglecting my invite yet my presence remains, no fault of their own, not even mine cause family is the forced parts of us, born out of a magnetic field, living by its own accord.

I point my finger as a warning sign these parts don't speak back there not here to argue with self. They say mission declared. They say mission to be delivered, no option just motion… they said. The pain in my lower back is supported by bricks of the known, only to be seated on the stoops of the unknown, resting in the melody of peace playing in my mind. Taking a deep breath. I take a quick peek through the window the ripped curtains giving me grace to do so. I take one last look at my mom and dad laughing and enjoying the party, I shake my head the perfect threesome develops when the other partner is whiskey, which has always had to unique ability to uncover the source of light between the two equivalent to a grain of sand, ranking below in quality.

Whiskey, the ability to cut on a flickering light in the urgent way one hits a flashlight against the palm of the hand, waiting for the one successful smack, flicking the light on leading to a moment of salvageable material. Introducing those so desirable defeated sparks seeming to cradle the shared responsibility of neglect that robbed my parents long before the bumping 'n' gridin' created my little sister and I.

The thundering and raindrops began to shower me as my tears matched the momentum of the raindrops hitting the back stoops. I remain, as if stuck, bonded to the inside looking at outside tragedy. The sudden ring of my phone woke me from my trance, peering down looking at my daughter's picture highlight the front screen of my phone. I took a deep breath declined the call, rose to my feet, and yelled out to self, "I'm sorry!" I am so sorry; I rush to grab my pen writing at the top of my page.

Letter of Self Forgiveness

I forgive me for all the negative names I called me. Names that grew from soil designed to enrich seeds of anger, loneliness, pain no love. Little Me... Come here... no don't run. I'm not here to hurt you anymore... I'll wait... I won't rush you... Let me extend my right arm to you... oh you think I can't lift you and carry you back to me... cause all the weight your pain holds. I shift my entire body, so I am facing Little Me, I recognized so far, I been talking to you with my back turned. I must admit I'm a bit afraid to look at the physical appearance of Little Me. I need to look at him... A slow turn I am now looking at Little Me. My eyes scanning him up and down... lifting his small head, I know what you're thinking... No. I interrupted with a very tender voice. I'm not ashamed.

I look at the dirty sneakers you wear the stains outlining your clothes and for the first time, I'm not interested in listening in on the outside voices shouting the words prompting the definition of a hopeless child. Don't run let me caress your face Little Me. Slightly and gently lift your chin... grab my hand... still not sure? I only see one hand, please show me your other... for assurance... you understand right?

I smile... yes, I understand but I must warn you vision of my two hands has no leadership in defining everlasting protection. The very presence of me in this moment would not be possible without the source of the power and strength of Jesus. I'm no stronger than you Little Me. I'm here to hold your hand... walk with me. I'm not too much for you... I don't want to. Remember it's too much for me, but never too much for him. Ready to go on stage... I don't know... me either... I'm nervous... me too. Little Me looks up at me, can you tie my shoe before we go out there... I got you... I love you... I love you too.